W9-BVM-516

Weekly Reader Children's Book Club *presents*

A LITTLE OLD MAN

by Natalie Norton

pictures by Will Huntington

RAND McNALLY & COMPANY

Copyright © 1959 by Rand McNally & Company
Copyright 1959 under International Copyright Union by Rand McNally & Company
All rights reserved   •   Printed in U.S.A.

Library of Congress Catalog Card Number: 59-6968

Weekly Reader Children's Book Club Edition
Primary Division

FOR SIMON AND PETER

Once there was a little old man who
lived in a little house on a little island
in the middle of a great big ocean.

He lived all by himself.
He was a smiling little old man with
no hair at all on the top of his head.
But he did have a nice white beard.

Every day after he had washed
himself and dressed himself, he cooked
his own breakfast. He thought it would
be fun if he had someone to eat with.

He was a very busy little old man.
After breakfast, he swept his little
house inside.

And then he worked outside.
Sometimes he worked in his garden.

Sometimes he worked on the roof of his little house.

Sometimes he went fishing in his
rowboat.

And caught fish to fry in his
frying pan.

But the little old man had no one to talk to and sometimes he was sad.

He thought he would be very happy
if he had a cat.

At night he dreamed of cats—big cats
and little cats, black cats and gray
cats, and sometimes little kittens.

One morning when the little old man
woke up he heard rain splashing
on his roof.

And when he went outdoors, the wind was blowing and the ocean waves were getting bigger and bigger.

Suddenly a huge wave came and
carried the little old man's little house
right out into the ocean.

No one ever came for the boat. And
the little old man was never sad or
lonely again.

And caught fish to fry in the
frying pan.

They went fishing in the little boat.

And painted it on the outside.

And so he and the cat and the four
kittens lived together on the boat.
They swept it on the inside.

The little old man was as happy as
any little old man could be.

Out from under the stove came one, two, three, four kittens.

Purrp! Purrp! Purrp! Purrp!

And then the little old man heard a
sound. Purrp! Out from under the stove
came a cat!

The little old man looked all around
and said: "Oh my, what a wonderful
house this would be. I will live in it
until the people who own it come for it."

And a kitchen as neat as could be.

Then the little old man went inside.
He found a bedroom with bunks
at the sides.

He walked all around the outside. It
was a big boat, bigger than the little
old man's house. And on the deck was
a little boat, smaller than the little old
man's rowboat.

The wind and the waves pushed the boat right up onto the island where his little house used to be.

When the rain stopped raining and the wind stopped blowing, the little old man went to see what the boat was like.

No, it was a boat.

Or could he? There was something
far out in the ocean. Could it be his
house?

There the waves tossed it and the wind blew it until the little old man could no longer see his little house.